Secret Kingdom

Special thanks to Linda Chapman

ORCHARD BOOKS
Carmelite House
50 Victoria Embankment
London EC4Y 0DZ
Orchard Books Australia
Level 17/207 Kent Street, Sydney, NSW 2000
A Paperback Original

First published in 2015 by Orchard Books

Text © Hothouse Fiction Limited 2015

Illustrations © Orchard Books 2015

A CIP catalogue record for this book is available
from the British Library.

ISBN 978 1 40834 008 0

1 3 5 7 9 10 8 6 4 2

Printed in Great Britain

MIX
Paper from
responsible sources
FSC® C104740
www.fsc.org

The paper and board used in this book are made from wood from responsible sources

Orchard Books is an imprint of Hachette Children's Group and published by the Watts
Publishing Group Limited, an Hachette UK company.
www.hachette.co.uk

Series created by Hothouse Fiction
www.hothousefiction.com

Genie Wish

ROSIE BANKS

ORCHARD

This is the Secret Kingdom

The Brilliant Bazaar

Contents

Glittering Sand

"Isn't this fun?" Jasmine Smith said happily to her two best friends, Ellie Macdonald and Summer Hammond. The three girls were spending the afternoon making pictures using some tubes of sparkly, coloured sand and glue that Ellie had bought at the craft shop.

Ellie nodded. She had drawn an outline in glue and sprinkled sand on. Now she gently shook the loose bits of sand on to the newspaper covering the table. "I love making sand pictures."

"You love anything to do with art," Summer said with a smile. "And you're so good at it too. Your picture is amazing."

"Thanks," said Ellie. Summer and Jasmine had both made quite simple pictures with the sand and glue – Summer's was a cat and Jasmine's was a microphone – but Ellie's was far more complicated. She had drawn a beautiful palace with pink pointy turrets and a grand entrance.

"It's just like King Merry's palace in the Secret Kingdom," Jasmine said, looking over Ellie's shoulder.

"Shh!" Ellie said. "Mum might hear." The three friends shared an incredible

secret. They were the only people that
knew about the Secret Kingdom – an
amazing, magical land that was filled
with wonderful creatures like pixies,
unicorns, mermaids, elves and fairies. It
was ruled by the jolly King Merry, and
Ellie, Summer and Jasmine had visited it
lots of times.

"Do you think King Merry has worked
out where the last two Enchanted
Objects are yet?" Jasmine whispered.

"Probably not, or he would have sent us
a message in the Magic Box," said Ellie.

"I hope he figures out where they are
soon," said Summer. "Then we can go
and help him find them!"

The girls were in the middle of one of
their Secret Kingdom adventures. The
king's wicked sister, Queen Malice, had

cast a horrible spell, which was making
all the magic in the Secret Kingdom
slowly drain away. The only way to
stop her was to find the four special
Enchanted Objects that were hidden
around the kingdom. Together the objects'
magic could reverse the queen's nasty
spell   but time was running out. If they
didn't find them all before the sand ran
through Queen Malice's cursed hourglass
then all the magic in the Secret Kingdom
would vanish forever.

"At least we've found the Charmed
Heart and the Silver Shell," said Ellie. "I
wonder what the last two objects will be."

"And *where* they'll be," added Jasmine.

"Perhaps we should go and check on
the Magic Box to see if there's a message
from King Merry," said Summer. "It's in

your room, isn't it, Ellie?"

"Yes, inside my wardrobe under some—" Ellie broke off as Molly, her four-year-old sister, came charging into the kitchen. Her green eyes were wide and her red curls were bouncing on her shoulders.

"Ellie!" she gasped. "I just went into your room and there's a light shining from your wardrobe! Quickly! You've got to come and see!"

Ellie, Summer and Jasmine jumped up in alarm. The glow

Molly saw must have been coming from the Magic Box – it always sparkled and shone when King Merry sent them a message.

"A shining light? In my wardrobe? Oh, don't worry about that, Moll," Ellie said

hurriedly. "It's just…just…"

"I bet it's that torch I lent you, Ellie," Jasmine said quickly. "Do you remember? You put it into your bag when we were at school."

"That's right," said Ellie gratefully. "I must have left it switched on. Silly me."

"Oh," said Molly, disappointed at such a boring explanation.

"Hey, Molly have you seen our pictures and this cool glitter?" said Summer, holding up some pink sparkly sand. She had two little brothers and she knew how much they loved anything to do with arts and crafts.

"Oh, wow!' said Molly, going over. "It's really pretty."

"Would you like to make a picture?" Ellie said. "Maybe you could draw a person or do some patterns."

"Oh, yes please!" said Molly.

"Here you go then," said Ellie, putting some paper and glue in front of her. "Use the glue to make your picture and then scatter the sand on top. Just don't make too much mess or Mum will get cross. We'll just pop upstairs to turn that torch off and then we'll come back and help you."

Ellie, Summer and Jasmine hurried out of the kitchen and up the stairs.

"It must be the Magic Box glowing!" hissed Ellie, leaping the stairs two at a time. The others followed her. As they raced into her bedroom, they saw that Molly was right. A light was shining out from the cracks in Ellie's wardrobe door. Jasmine quickly shut the bedroom

door behind them while Ellie ran to her
wardrobe and opened it.

Golden light spilled out into the room.
Ellie took out the Magic Box. It was
sparkling brightly, and the girls saw
that swirly writing had appeared in its
mirrored lid.

"It's a message from King Merry. What
does it say?" Summer asked excitedly.

They all knelt on the rug, and Ellie read out the riddle.

"Please come to a market in a desert that glows
With genies and camels and snake-charming shows."

There was a bright flash and suddenly the lid of the box flew open. A scroll of

paper shot into the air and unfolded itself before floating down to the rug. It was a beautiful map that showed the whole of the Secret Kingdom. All the brightly painted pictures on it moved. The girls knew they had to use it to solve the riddle.

"Let's see," Ellie said, leaning over the map. "So we're looking for a market in a glowing desert. Can anyone see anything like that on here?"

They scanned all the pictures. There were so many beautiful places to see – Clearsplash Waterfall, Dream Dale, Magic Mountain…

"Here!" Jasmine said, spotting a stretch of silver sand in the far east of the kingdom. There were five pink camels walking in a line across the sand. "Look, this place is called the Silver Desert!"

"And there's something in the middle of it," said Ellie, pointing to a group of low white buildings and palm trees. She read out the label. "*The Brilliant Bazaar.* Oh." Her face fell. "It's not a market."

"But it is!" said Summer. "I've read about bazaars. They're like a mixture of a market and a fair. They're usually in places like Egypt, and they have lots of different stalls and side shows, like snake charming and people walking across hot coals."

"Can you imagine how amazing a bazaar in the Secret Kingdom must be?" said Jasmine. "There's bound to be all sorts of magical things happening."

"I bet the Brilliant Bazaar is the place we're looking for," said Ellie.

"Oh, I hope so!" said Summer. "We've never been to that bit of the Secret Kingdom before."

"Let's see if we're right," said Jasmine.

She put her hands on the box. Ellie and Summer copied her and together they cried, "The Brilliant Bazaar!"

Three silver sparks shot out of the box. All three sparks faded and vanished with a faint popping noise. The girls looked at each other in surprise. Normally there was a bright flash and their friend Trixibelle, the royal pixie appeared.

"What's going—" Ellie broke off with a squeak as a cloud of silver glitter suddenly erupted out of the box like a tornado. The glitter shot upwards and then fell down over the girls, covering them from head to toe.

Ellie spluttered and wiped the glitter off her face. Jasmine and Summer giggled. They were coated with glitter too.

They heard a peal of tinkly laughter coming from inside the box.

"Whoops! I didn't mean to make quite so much glitter come out! Sorry, girls! My magic's still misbehaving – but at least the Magic Box seems to be working a bit better than the last few times I've come to fetch you!" A tiny pixie zoomed out of the box on a green leaf, her blonde curls bouncing as she moved. The leaf whizzed round the girls' heads and came to a stop, hovering in front of their noses. "Hello, girls!" the pixie said, waving.

"Trixi!" the girls cried. "Hello."

Trixi swooped over to kiss each of them on the nose. "I'm sorry again that I

made you so
sparkly!"

"We don't
mind," said
Jasmine,
grinning.
"We like
being
sparkly."

"Though
I'm not sure
my mum will like
quite so much glitter on
my bedroom floor!" said Ellie.

"Don't worry. I think I can deal with that!" Trixi tapped the green ring on her finger. There was a flash and the glitter vanished, leaving the room just as before. "That's better. Now, are you ready to come to the Silver Desert?"

"Yes!" the three girls said.

Trixi beamed. "Wonderful. King Merry is waiting at the Brilliant Bazaar for you. He has heard that one of the Enchanted Objects might be hidden somewhere there."

The girls grabbed each other's hands.

"Are you ready?" Trixi said. They nodded, so she tapped her magic ring again and called out a spell.

"Please take us to the
Brilliant Bazaar
Arriving on camels, travelling afar!"

More silver sand shot out of the centre of Trixi's ring and swirled around the girls in a glittering cloud, lifting them up and whisking them away. Round and round they twirled, until they slowly started coming back down.

All three girls felt tingly with excitement. They were off to the Secret Kingdom!

The Brilliant Bazaar

Summer squeezed her eyes shut, but found she'd landed with a soft bump on to a heap of brightly coloured cushions. She blinked and sat up to see Ellie was sprawled on more cushions beside her. They were in some sort of strange golden carriage with a gauzy blue canopy over the top and a strange, pink, furry lump in the middle. Cushions surrounded

the lump and she and Ellie were now
wearing light, floaty clothes with golden
bangles around their arms. But where
were Jasmine and Trixi?

The carriage was moving a bit jerkily.
Summer stuck her head out of the
window to look around, and gasped.
"Ellie! We're on the back of a camel!"

The large camel had pink fur the
colour of candyfloss. Walking next to
it was another pink camel that had a
carriage on top of it, too. Jasmine looked
out of that carriage and waved.

"Summer! I'm over here with Trixi!
Where's Ellie?"

"Here!" Ellie poked her head out of the
window beside Summer. "Wow! Isn't this
amazing?" She straightened the sparkling
tiara on her head. The tiaras always

appeared when the girls were transported to the Secret Kingdom. They showed everyone the girls met that they were Very Important Friends of King Merry.

"It's incredible!" said Jasmine.

Trixi came flying out of the window of Jasmine's carriage on her leaf. "Do you like the camels, girls?"

"They're lovely," said Summer, stroking her camel's soft pink fur. "Thank you for giving us a lift," she called to it.

The camel snorted happily as it plodded on across the shining sand with its ears pricked. It seemed much more cheerful than the grumpy camels Summer was used to seeing in Honeyvale Zoo back at home, but then it *was* a Secret Kingdom camel!

"It's really warm here," said Jasmine

fanning her face. The sun was shining brightly above them in the blue sky, making the silver sand glitter and shine.

"We'll be at the Brilliant Bazaar soon," said Trixi. "Look."

She pointed ahead and there were some bright white buildings just like they had seen on the magic map. It was a town

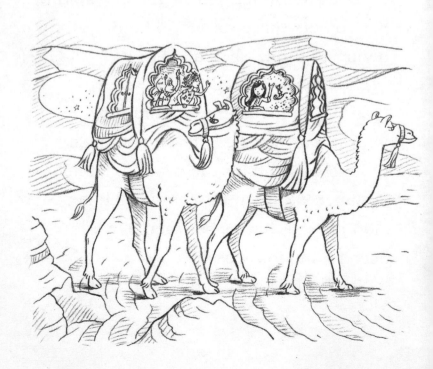

with a big arched entrance to it. As the camels plodded closer, the girls heard noises drifting out through the gateway – there were pipes playing, people calling out, animals honking and braying. A spicy scent like cinnamon and nutmeg caught at their nostrils.

They reached the gateway and the

camels stopped. A set of steps magically unfolded from each carriage, allowing the girls to climb down easily.

"Come on!" said Trixi, flying ahead of them. "We must find King Merry!"

The girls said thank you to the camels and then ran through the archway. They found themselves in a big market square with narrow streets leading off it in all directions.

"Welcome to the Brilliant Bazaar!" said Trixi.

"It's amazing!" said Jasmine, looking this way and that. It was so noisy and there was so much to see she could hardly take it all in. Elves and brownies were hurrying about, some wheeling carts, others carrying boxes. There were brightly coloured chickens pecking in the dust, lilac donkeys being herded through the streets and stalls where stripy sweets, fresh fruit and sparkling jewels were being sold. A group of belly-dancers were dancing in a line. Jasmine wished she could go and join them!

Summer spotted a snake-charmer

sitting cross-legged
in front of a
large wicker
basket, playing
an instrument
that looked
a bit like a
flute, and near
to him was a
man holding a golden
bird with jewel-like eyes and long tail
feathers. "That's a *phoenix*!" Summer
exclaimed.

"Now, where is King Merry?" said Trixi
anxiously. "I asked him to meet us right
here…"

"Yoo-hoo!" They turned and saw a
small, round figure hurrying through the
crowds towards them, waving. excitedly

"Yoo-hoo, my friends!"

"King Merry!" Jasmine exclaimed in delight.

The king was wearing baggy white trousers and a big white shirt. He had a golden sash around his ample tummy, a golden cloak and golden slippers with curled up toes. His crown was falling to one side on his grey curly hair, but his eyes were twinkling kindly, just as they always did.

"My dear, dear friends," he cried. "Oh,

I'm so glad you're here!"

They all hugged him.

"It's lovely to see you, King Merry," said Ellie. "We came as soon as we saw the Magic Box's message."

"Excellent," said the king, pushing his little half moon spectacles back up his nose. "There's simply no time to waste. All the magic in the land is going so wonky at the moment. Look around, you can see for yourselves!" He swept his arm round the crowded square. "Oh, my dreadful sister has a lot to answer for."

It took the girls a moment to work out what he meant, but then they started to notice things that they hadn't spotted at first. Elf children were buying flavour-changing sweets and then spitting them out, complaining that they tasted sour. A

brownie standing by a wagon of golden
apples was wringing his hands as the
fruit went dull
and mouldy
before
his eyes.
Two elves
were trying
to control a
magic carpet,
holding onto it
with a rope as it
bucked and plunged
around them like a
wild horse, and the snakes in
the snake-charmer's basket kept popping
their heads out and then diving straight
back inside.

"Oh dear," said Jasmine. "I see what

you mean, King Merry. All the magic
seems to be going wrong."

"It's all horribly out of control," said
King Merry. "We have to stop my sister's
wicked spell."

"Trixi said you think that one of the
Enchanted Objects might be here," Ellie
said hopefully.

"Yes, I was told that there's a genie
here who may be able to help us," replied
King Merry. "She's a Wish Genie called
Gina. She comes to the Brilliant Bazaar
once a year to do a special magical
Smoke Dance. The crowds flock to watch
her. I believe she's about to perform
somewhere in the bazaar."

"Then let's find her," said Jasmine
eagerly. She jumped as one of the snakes
in the basket turned into a colourful

parrot and erupted out of the basket with a surprised squawk. "There's really not a second to waste!"

Gina the Wish Genie

The girls and King Merry quickly set off across the square, with Trixi flying beside them. As the people in the bazaar saw the king, they gasped and started bowing and curtseying.

"Oh, no, no, it's quite all right. Please don't worry about all that," said King Merry, looking rather embarrassed. "We're just trying to find Gina the Wish Genie. Have you seen her?"

"This way, Your Majesty. This way!
She's in the Silver Square," called a
group of elves, pointing them in the right
direction.

The girls followed King Merry down
a narrow alleyway with tall houses on
either side.

"So, does Gina the Wish Genie
live inside a lamp?" Summer asked,
remembering the stories she had read
about genies. They always seemed to be
trapped in lamps, only coming out to
grant three wishes when the lamp was
rubbed.

"Not any more," said King Merry.
"Once, long ago, before I was king, when
King Moody was the ruler, all the genies
were trapped in lamps. King Moody kept
them as his servants." The plump little

king shook his head. "Crowns
and coronations, isn't that awful?
Anyway, one of the first things I did
when I became ruler was to set all the
genies free."

"You're so lovely, King Merry," Summer
said, squeezing his hand.

King Merry's cheeks turned pink with
delight. "That's very nice of you to say so,
my dear. You are too!"

The winding alleyway led into in a
second square, where more strange things
were going on. Another golden phoenix
on a perch was trying to sing for the
crowd but instead of beautiful notes
flooding out of its beak, it was making
a barking noise like a dog, and a lilac
donkey was looking very alarmed as
big wings started to grow on its back.

But most people were clustering round
something in the centre of the square,
where there was the sound of strange,
mysterious music playing. Trixi flew
up higher to see over the
crowd.

"It's Gina the
Wish Genie!" she
cried. "I can see
her! There's a
stage for her
show in the
centre of the
square." She
tapped her ring
and her voice came
out like she was speaking
into a megaphone. "Make
way for His Majesty King Merry,

please! Make way!"

Seeing the king, the crowds quickly parted to let him through.

"It's King Merry," the girls heard some little gnomes whispering to each other. "And he's got his special friends with him. Look, you can see their tiaras!"

In the centre of the square there was a silver stage, and standing on it was a beautiful girl with green skin and long dark hair. She was wearing purple chiffon pantaloons and a sparkly top. When she saw King Merry, her eyes widened. "Your Majesty! I'm so honoured to meet you." She put her hands together and bowed low. Her voice was soft and musical, her eyes slightly slanting like a cat's.

"You must be Gina the Wish Genie," said King Merry.

The genie girl nodded. "I am, Your Majesty."

"I'm delighted to meet you, my dear. I've been told you might be able to help me."

"Of course, Your Majesty. I will do everything in my power to help you," said Gina. "Please come into my tent, and you can tell me how I may be of assistance." She gestured to a green-and-blue silk tent at the back of the stage.

They all followed her inside. There were giant silken cushions lining the edges, and the fabric of the tent muffled the noise from the square.

Trixi tapped her ring and conjured a little throne for the king to sit on.

"Please, be seated," the genie said to the girls, waving her hands at the cushions. "I'm afraid, although I know you are important friends of King Merry, I do not know your names."

"I am Jasmine, this is Ellie and Summer," said Jasmine.

"Now, Gina, my dear," said King Merry. "Have you heard that my sister is causing trouble again?"

Gina nodded. "I have. Everywhere I go people are talking about Queen Malice's horrible spell. I have been very lucky that my own magic hasn't been affected."

"Why hasn't it?" Ellie said in surprise.

"Because of this." Gina reached into the pocket of her baggy trousers and pulled out a golden lamp. It was

intricately engraved and shone brightly. "The Glitter Lamp. It belonged to one of my ancestors and was passed down to me. I believe it is the most powerful magical lamp ever made."

Summer caught her breath and looked at King Merry. "Do you think it might be one of the Enchanted Objects, King Merry?"

Gina looked puzzled.

"I think it may well be," said King Merry. He quickly explained to Gina what the Enchanted Objects were.

Gina's eyes lit up with understanding. "So you need the Glitter Lamp to help defeat Queen Malice? Then here, King Merry. Please take it." She held it out.

"Thank you, Gina," said the king. "That is very kind of you. I will return it to you just as soon as we have broken this dreadful spell."

Jasmine beamed. "I can't believe finding this Enchanted Object has been so easy!"

"It's been the easiest yet. Now we've

just got one more object left to find, and we can stop Queen Malice's spell," said Ellie happily.

CRACK!

Suddenly, there was a huge clap of thunder. Outside the tent there was the sound of shouting.

"What's happening?" said Gina, jumping to her feet in alarm.

A loud, familiar cackle echoed around the square.

"Oh no – it's Queen Malice!" exclaimed Jasmine, looking outside the tent. She pulled back the flap, looking at the others anxiously.

Tall, bony Queen Malice was swooping down towards the stage on the back of a giant black hawk with red eyes. Her hair frizzed out around her face, and she gripped her thunderstaff in one hand. As the hawk landed, Queen Malice pointed her staff at the tent.

"Come out, genie," she hissed. "And give me that Glitter Lamp – or I'll come in there and *take* it from you!"

A Wicked Plan

Jasmine glared. She wasn't afraid of Queen Malice! Pushing back the flap, she marched out of the tent. "Go away!" she shouted to the nasty queen.

"You're not having the Glitter Lamp," added Ellie, running out to stand beside her friend.

Summer joined them. "We won't let you take it!" She put her hands on her hips. She was a bit more frightened of Queen Malice than Jasmine and Ellie, but she was determined not to show it.

Gina hurried out too, with King Merry and Trixi. She had the lamp in her arms. "The girls are right. I'm never going to let you have this lamp, Queen Malice, so you might as well just leave us alone!"

"Very well," Queen Malice said. "I'll leave!" She yanked on the hawk's bridle, and kicked its feathery sides. It gave a squawk, and almost before anyone realised what was happening it flew straight at Gina. As it shot past her, Queen Malice reached out and grabbed the golden lamp from her hands. The evil queen cackled delightedly as the hawk swooped upwards above the tent. Gina cried out in surprise and dismay.

"My lamp!" The Wish Genie gasped.

"Well, I did say I'd leave!" sneered Queen Malice. "But I'll be taking the Glitter Lamp with me!"

"Give that lamp back, sister!" shouted King Merry, shaking his fist.

"Never!" replied the queen. "And now that I think of it, you can say goodbye to your green-faced friend too!"

She pointed her staff at Gina and shouted out a spell.

"Glitter Lamp, trap this genie inside,
In your depths she'll now reside.
Her magic's strong, but now bound
to me,
She won't stop my spell, even if she
breaks free."

A thunderbolt shot out of the end of
Queen Malice's staff and hit
Gina. The genie cried
out in alarm as she
was turned into a
smoky green figure.
Then, before their
eyes, Gina was
sucked up into
the spout of
the lamp!

"No!"
gasped Summer.

Trixi flew her leaf straight at Queen
Malice and tried to grab the lamp.
The queen swiped at her with her
thunderstaff.

"Stay away, little pixie!" she hissed.
"The lamp is no good to you now.

It cannot be used as one of the
Enchanted Objects while it has the genie
inside!" She threw the lamp high in the
air. As it spun there, Queen Malice fired a
thunderbolt at it.

CRACK!

The lamp
vanished.

"What
have you
done, sister?" said
King Merry, aghast.
Queen Malice
looked delighted with
herself. "I have hidden
the lamp where you
will never get it, my
dear brother. Why, you're

so stupid that even if I gave you a clue as to where it was, I bet you would never find it."

King Merry spluttered, but Jasmine spoke quickly. "You're right, Queen Malice, you're so much cleverer than we are."

Summer and Ellie looked at her in astonishment.

"I'm sure that even if you gave us a load of clues we'd never be able to find it," Jasmine went on. "You've beaten us for sure this time."

"What are you saying, Jasmine?" hissed Summer.

"Ssh," Jasmine whispered, her eyes on Queen Malice.

"I really have beaten you this time, haven't I?" the Queen crowed. "Oh, I'm so clever! Well, all I can say is that you'd have to be very QUICK if you wanted to rescue your friend. Or all the SAND in the magic hourglass will run out. *Then* all the good magic of the Secret Kingdom will drain away too, and I shall be the ruler! And you, brother…" She pointed her staff at King Merry. "You'll be my prisoner and live in the SWAMP around Thunder Castle forever!"

Cackling triumphantly, she dug her heels hard into the hawk's sides. They all watched in dismay as it flapped off, carrying Queen Malice away.

Ellie broke the silence. "What are we going to do now?"

"We have to find Gina as quickly as we can," said Trixi.

"We absolutely must," said King Merry,

his eyes filling with tears. "Oh, the
poor girl."

"But we don't have any idea where
Queen Malice has sent the Glitter Lamp,"
said Ellie.

"If only she *had* given us a clue," said
Trixi with a sigh.

"Oh, but she did," said Jasmine. "Didn't
you hear?"

They all looked at her. "What do you
mean?" Summer asked.

"Do you remember when I told Queen
Malice that she was cleverer than us and
that even if she gave us lots of clues we
wouldn't work out where the lamp was?"

"Yes," said Summer. "I thought that was
odd."

"I was trying to make her think she
could give us a clue and it wouldn't

matter – and I think she gave us *three*!"

"Three clues?" said Ellie.

Jasmine nodded. "She said three words really strangely, as if they were important. She said we'd have to be very QUICK or all the SAND in the magic hourglass would run out, and King Merry would be her prisoner in the SWAMP around Thunder Castle. I think Queen Malice really does think she's cleverer than us, and wanted to prove it by giving us clues she never thought we'd understand."

"What? QUICK and SAND and SWAMP are clues?" said Ellie.

Jasmine nodded.

"The Quicksand Swamp!" gasped Trixi, nearly falling off her leaf in excitement. "Of course! There's a place called Quicksand Swamp in the Silver Desert."

"Sceptres and orbs!" said King Merry. "That must be where she's sent Gina."

"Oh, Jasmine, you're brilliant!" said Summer hugging her.

"Well, we don't know if I'm right yet," said Jasmine modestly.

"There's only one way to find out!" said Ellie.

Trixi turned to King Merry. "Why don't I go with the girls to Quicksand Swamp, while you stay here and try to calm everyone down, Your Majesty?"

The people in the square were clustered together anxiously after Queen Malice's visit. Some were crying and all of them looked worried.

"Very well," said King Merry. "I shall talk to everyone here and explain what is happening. Hurry back as quickly as you can, my dears."

"We will – and hopefully we'll bring Gina and the Glitter Lamp back with us!" said Jasmine.

King Merry set off towards the stage. "Friends, my dear friends!" he called to the crowds. "Please gather around! Let

me explain what has been happening…"

"Can you use your magic to take us to Quicksand Swamp, Trixi?" Jasmine asked while King Merry spoke to the crowd.

Trixi nodded quickly, and the girls held each other's hands. Trixi tapped her ring.

"Pixie magic, take us to the quicksand,
Set us down close to it, but on
dry land."

Nothing happened. Trixi tapped her ring and said the spell again, but still nothing happened. She looked at the girls in alarm. "My magic's still not working properly. It won't take us to the Quicksand Swamp after all. Now what are we going to do?"

A Magic Ride

The girls looked at one another in alarm. "If Trixi's magic can't transport us, we're going to have to find another way to get to Quicksand Swamp," said Jasmine.

"We could ride the camels again?" Ellie suggested.

"That would take too long," said Trixi. "It's a whole day's camel ride away. The only way of getting there quickly is by magic. Oh, if only we could fly…"

Summer frowned. An idea buzzed about in the back of her brain. Suddenly the image of two elves trying to control a magic carpet popped into her mind. "A flying carpet!" she exclaimed. "We saw one in the first square we went into! Why don't we find out if we can borrow it?"

"Perfect!" said Jasmine.

Summer started to run through the crowds. The others raced after her, with Trixi flying behind them. Dodging round donkeys and swerving past snake charmers, they sprinted back into the first square. The two elves were still there with the flying carpet. They had tied it to a wooden post and it was flying around it in circles.

"Please, we need your help!" Summer panted. "Can we borrow your carpet?"

"It's to help King Merry," said Ellie.

"To help the whole kingdom," Jasmine added.

The elves looked surprised. "Of course you can borrow it," said one.

"Here." The other elf untied the carpet. The rope was attached to its tassles along one side. "But be careful. It's not behaving very well today. Try to tell it where you want to go and use this rope to help guide it. Down, carpet. Down!"

The carpet sank down to the floor. Jasmine and Ellie and Summer climbed onto it and sat down cross-legged.

"To the Quicksand Swamp please, carpet!" Jasmine instructed.

The carpet quivered and suddenly rose up into the air with all three of them on it.

"Whoa!" gasped Ellie, grabbing

Summer as they went up and up. She didn't like heights!

Trixi flew up beside them on her pixie leaf. "Come on, carpet. Follow me!"

She shot away, and the flying carpet

followed. Jasmine whooped in delight as
they flew through the arched gateway
and out across the glittering silver sand of
the desert.

"Isn't this amazing?" said Jasmine.

Ellie groaned. Her eyes were tightly
shut. "Just tell me when we're there!"

The carpet raced over the desert
following Trixi. Summer had a feeling it
was delighted to be out and flying fast.

They flew on and on, until Trixi gave a
shout. "Look! Here's the swamp!"

Jasmine and Summer shaded their eyes.
They could see a large swamp of darker
sand below them. Surrounding the swamp
were bushes, and the occasional tree. In
the very centre of the swamp was a tree
stump with something gold and glittery
resting on it.

"It's the Glitter Lamp!" cried Summer.

Ellie opened her eyes. She was so thrilled to see the lamp that she forgot all about being scared. "Let's swoop down and get it."

"Take us to the lamp, please," Jasmine said to the flying carpet. But it just flew round in circles.

"Down!" said Jasmine.

The carpet dropped down, but then swerved to the outside of the swamp and stopped dead about a metre from the ground. Jasmine pulled the rope, but the carpet shook itself as if it was a stubborn horse shaking its head, and refused to move.

"It doesn't seem to want to go to the tree stump," said Jasmine.

Trixi flew up to them. "Oh dear. It

must be because its magic isn't working properly. You'd better not insist or it might tip you into the swamp!"

None of them liked that idea. The swamp oozed and bubbled slightly.

"How are we going to get the lamp?"

said Ellie, looking across at the tree stump in desperation.

"I could fly over there, but it's too big for me to carry, and my ring isn't working properly so I don't think I can make it smaller," Trixi said.

Jasmine frowned. "There has to be some way of getting through the swamp."

"There isn't," said Trixi. "The quicksand would suck you under straight away."

The girls' eyes met. What were they going to do?

Summer looked longingly at the glittering lamp. "If only we could just wish it over here."

Trixi gasped and turned an excited loop-the-loop. "But we can! If I fly over there and rub the lamp, then Gina will come out and grant me three wishes. I can wish for the lamp to come over here."

"Perfect!" said Jasmine. "Go for it, Trixi!"

Trixi zoomed over the quicksand and hovered beside the lamp. Leaning over, she rubbed it with her hand. Sparkles ran across the lamp's golden surface, and suddenly a stream of green smoke shot out of the spout.

"Gina!" exclaimed the girls as the smoke formed into the shape of the genie girl, her legs trailing down inside the spout.

"You found me!" Gina cried in delight.

"Yes," called
Jasmine. "And
now we're going
to use Trixi's
three wishes to
free you and get the
lamp back to King
Merry."

"Oh, thank
you!" Gina
clasped her
hands together.
"Wish away, Trixi!"

"I wish—" the pixie began, but just as
she spoke, a large grey raindrop came
hurtling down towards Trixi's leaf. "Eek!"
she squealed, dodging out of the way just
in time.

The girls heard jeering laughter

overhead and looked up.

"It's Queen Malice's Storm Sprites!" gasped Jasmine, as five sprites swooped down on their leathery bat-like wings. The Storm Sprites were Queen Malice's horrible servants.

"And they've got their misery drops with them!" Ellie called. "Watch out, Trixi!"

"Splat the pixie! Get her!" shouted the Storm Sprites gleefully.

Trixi zoomed this way and that as the sprites chucked their drops at her.

"Leave Trixi alone!" shouted Summer furiously. Anyone who got hit by a misery drop always felt miserable for hours.

"Splat those pesky girls too!" cackled the sprites. "Splish! Splash! We're going to make you so sad you forget all about that sparkly lamp."

They started throwing drops at the girls.

"They're going to hit us!" gasped Ellie, ducking as a misery drop flew past them.

Trixi flew back to Gina. "I've got a wish!" she said hurriedly. "I wish that all the misery drops would vanish!"

"Your wish is granted!" cried Gina quickly, clapping her hands. There was a bright green flash, and all the misery drops disappeared.

"You meanies!" shrieked the sprites angrily. "You've spoiled our fun."

The Storm Sprites flew at Trixi and the lamp with their bony fingers outstretched. Trixi tried to get away, but one of the sprites caught the corner of her leaf. It tipped up, and Trixi squealed, tumbling down onto the quicksand.

"Help!" she shrieked as the sand started sucking her down into its silvery depths. Her little arms flailed. "Help me, please! I'm sinking!"

Wishing Magic

"Trixi!" cried Summer, Ellie and Jasmine.

Jasmine didn't stop to think. She leapt off the flying carpet, her eyes trained on Trixi's tiny figure struggling in the swamp. "It's OK, Trixi. I'll save you!"

"Don't come in!" gasped Trixi as she floundered in the quicksand. "You'll sink too!"

Jasmine grabbed a branch from the ground and lay down on her tummy at the edge of the sand. The Storm Sprites were flapping about overhead, cackling and jeering, but she ignored them. She wriggled forwards, stretching the branch out as far as she could towards Trixi. But it just wasn't quite long enough to reach the poor little pixie.

Ellie and Summer jumped from the

flying carpet too and raced over.

"Trixi, use another of your wishes," shouted Summer, seeing that Gina was still hovering, attached to the lamp. "Use it to wish yourself out of there."

Trixi gave her a grateful look. "Of course! Gina, I wish I was out of this quicksand and back on my leaf!" she gasped.

"Your wish is granted!" declared Gina

quickly, clapping her hands.

There was a green flash and suddenly Trixi shot out of the swamp, somersaulted through the air and landed on her leaf. It carried her safely over to the three girls. Trixi was pale and trembling. "That was horrible," she said, dusting the quicksand off her legs and arms.

"You're safe now," Summer told her.

"But I've used up another wish," said Trixi, her big eyes filling with tears.

"Girls! Help!" They heard Gina cry out, and looked round. The Storm Sprites had swooped down again, and one of them had grabbed the Glitter Lamp with Gina still hovering from the spout.

"You're coming with us, silly green genie!" the Storm Sprite crowed. "We're taking you to Queen Malice."

"Stop it! Bring her back!" shouted Ellie.
"No!" shrieked the sprite, flying higher.
"Make a wish, Trixi!" Jasmine cried.
"But what do I wish for?" said Trixi

in alarm. "If I wish for Gina to be freed then the sprites will take the empty Glitter Lamp to Queen Malice, and we'll lose it. But if I wish for the lamp to come to us, then Gina will be stuck inside it, so the lamp won't be any good as an Enchanted Object – and I won't have any wishes left to free her."

The sprite had already started flapping away, taking Gina with him.

"Just wish for the lamp to be back here with us," said Ellie. "We can't let them take it. At least we'll have both Gina and the lamp then, even if Gina is still trapped."

"We'll have to find another way to get her out," said Summer.

Jasmine nodded. "Quick! Make the wish, Trixi!"

"OK. Here goes. I wish that the Glitter Lamp was back here with us…!" cried Trixi. Her eyes sparkled with an idea. "And a long, long way away from the Storm Sprites."

"Your wish is granted!" shouted Gina, clapping her hands.

FLASH!

Gina vanished into the lamp. It jerked itself out of the sprite's hands and flew through the air towards the girls.

Jasmine jumped up and caught it as the Storm Sprites howled in rage. But

before they could
do anything, a
mini tornado
came sweeping
across the sky
towards them. It
whisked them up in
its swirling depths.
The sprites tumbled
over and over as
the tornado
carried on its
way, taking
them off over
the horizon.

Trixi gave a relieved laugh. "Phew!"

"Well, I guess you did wish for the lamp
to be a long way away from the sprites!"
said Jasmine. "That was really clever,

Trixi. It must have been what made the tornado appear. Now they've gone, we can calm down and think about what to do next."

"We have to get Gina out of the lamp and make our way back to the Brilliant Bazaar as quickly as possible," said Ellie.

"But how?" said Summer. "Hang on!" she said suddenly. "Can't one of *us* just rub the lamp? Then when Gina comes out, we'll get another three wishes!"

"It won't work," said Trixi sadly. "You have to *find* the lamp first and then rub it to make the genie come out. And the lamp's already here in Jasmine's arms."

"Oh," said Summer, disappointed. It had seemed such a perfect solution.

"Then I guess we'd better use the flying carpet to get back to the bazaar and find

King Merry," said Jasmine.

"Where *is* the carpet?" Summer said.

They all looked round. The flying
carpet had gone.

"Oh no," said Jasmine.

But just then Ellie's sharp eyes spotted
some tassels poking out from behind
a bush. She gave a shout. "It's OK,
everyone! Look, it's over there, hiding
behind a bush."

They all hurried over to the flying
carpet.

"Found you!" Summer said to it. She
paused. "Hang on." She frowned, thinking
hard. The carpet had been hidden and
they had just found it. Maybe if the lamp
was hidden they could find that too…

"I know what we should do!" she said.
"Trixi! You can *hide* the lamp, then we

can find it and have our three wishes."

"Great plan," said Jasmine.

"Yes! That should work," said Trixi.

"But how will you lift it, Trixi?" asked Ellie.

"Hmm, let me see." Trixi tapped her ring. A cloud of green sparkles shot out.

The pixie beamed. "Hooray! I can
use my ring. It
must be working
because it's
so close to
the lamp,
which is full
of powerful
magic. Here goes.
Shut your eyes,
everyone."

Summer, Ellie and
Jasmine covered their
eyes. There was a moment's silence
and then they heard a whooshing
sound.

"You can look now," Trixi told them.

They all opened their eyes. The lamp
had gone.

Ellie grinned at the others. "It's time to play find-the-lamp!" she said.

Back to the Bazaar

Summer, Ellie and Jasmine started hunting around. Luckily, there were only a few possible hiding places – behind the tree trunks and in the bushes.

Summer quickly spotted a glint of gold coming from behind a cluster of shrubs. "There!" she said, pointing.

They all ran over and spotted the lamp.

"Found it!" Jasmine said, and reached

down to grab it, but Summer stopped her.

"If we pick it up together, then maybe we'll be able to make the three wishes together," she said.

"Good idea," said Ellie. "After three. One, two, three…"

They all put their hands on the lamp at the same time and lifted it off the ground. The lamp's carved surface glittered in the sunlight. Trixi flew her leaf over to them.

"Now you can rub it and have your

three wishes!"

The three girls rubbed the lamp.

WHOOSH!

Gina shot out of the spout, hovering in the air.

"Oh, I am glad to be out of there," she said in relief. "It's very dark and cramped inside. What is your wish?"

The three girls looked at each other.

"What do we wish for?" Summer said.

"Can we just wish that Queen Malice's spell on the Secret Kingdom is broken?" Ellie said hopefully. "That would solve everything!"

"I'd love to grant that wish, but I'm afraid can't," Gina said. "When Queen Malice imprisoned me, she said even if I was freed, my magic could never be used to break her spell. I'm bound by her magic now."

Ellie looked disappointed. "Oh."

"We must be able to use our wishes to help in some way," said Summer.

"Well, we must use one wish to free Gina, but first I think we should wish that we were all back at the Brilliant Bazaar with King Merry," said Jasmine. "We don't want to still be here if the Storm Sprites come back."

"Agreed," said Summer and Ellie.

Jasmine took a breath. She wanted to get the wish exactly right. "I wish—" she began – but just as she spoke, there was a crash of thunder.

The girls, Gina and Trixi looked up just in time to see Queen Malice swooping down towards them on her giant black hawk!

"Oh, no!" Trixi cried.

"Oh, *yes!*" Queen Malice retorted, her hawk screeching loudly as its wings flapped rapidly. "You may have thwarted my Storm Sprites, but now that lamp will be mine!"

Summer, Ellie and Jasmine looked at

one another, and then Ellie shouted, "Quick, Jasmine, make your wish!"

Jasmine nodded quickly, and then cried out, "I wish we were all safely away from Queen Malice, back at the Brilliant Bazaar, standing next to King Merry, with the lamp and Gina!"

Gina clapped her hands and there was a flash. "Your wish is granted!"

The world seemed to turn upside down and the girls tumbled over and over. They saw a spinning image of Queen Malice shaking her fist angrily, and then they heard the sound of people and animals, and smelt cinnamon and nutmeg. Their feet hit the ground and they opened their eyes. They were back in the Brilliant Bazaar, standing beside the stage, next to King Merry!

"My friends! You're back!" King Merry said in delight. He saw that Jasmine was holding the lamp with Gina floating out of the spout. "Oh, and you've found Gina and the Glitter Lamp!"

"Yes, King Merry," said Jasmine.

"We just need to make two more wishes, and then you can take the lamp back to the your palace to keep it safe," said Summer.

Jasmine handed the lamp to Ellie to make the next wish.

"OK, let me think…" Ellie looked at her friends, and then carefully said, "I wish that the Brilliant Bazaar was back to normal."

Gina grinned broadly, and then clapped her hands together.

Suddenly all around them, people exclaimed as everything in the bazaar started to change back to how it had been. The golden fruit on the stalls became perfect and juicy looking again, a phoenix started to sing a beautiful song, and the donkey lost its wings.

Children skipped round, laughing and dancing.

"Oh, my friends!" said King Merry to the girls. "You've made everyone in the Brilliant Bazaar happy again! Wonderful!"

"Just one more wish left," Trixi said, and Ellie handed Summer the lamp. They all looked at her.

"I wish…" Summer began quietly. Then she shouted, "I wish that Gina was free from the lamp!"

"Your wish is granted!" cried Gina gratefully, clapping her hands together one last time. There was a flash of bright light, and suddenly Gina was standing on the ground beside them, looking just like she had when they first met her.

"I'm free!" she cried spinning round in delight. She hugged all three girls. "Oh, thank you! Thank you so much!"

Summer gave King Merry the Glitter Lamp. "Now you can keep the lamp safe with the Charmed Heart and the Silver Shell, Your Majesty."

"I certainly will." King Merry took the lamp and tucked it carefully in the folds of his cloak.

The crowd began to chant. "Gina! Gina! Gina!"

King Merry turned to the Wish Genie. "I think everyone is very keen to see your special Smoke Dance, Gina, dear. It would be a simply wonderful way to celebrate the bazaar returning to normal. Will you perform it?"

"It would be my pleasure!" declared Gina happily.

She ran lightly up the steps that led to the stage and held out her hands. The crowd fell quiet. "Greetings. I am once more free from the lamp, thanks to the brave and kind actions of Trixibelle the royal pixie and King Merry's three Very

Important Friends – Jasmine, Summer and Ellie. I shall now perform my Smoke Dance in their honour, and in the king's honour too. Music please!" She clicked her fingers, and at the side of the stage three elves started playing their flutes.

Lilting notes filled the square and Gina waved her hands in front of her face. Rainbow-coloured streams of smoke floated from her fingers like magic ribbons. They surrounded her in glowing strands. Gina started to dance, twirling round the stage, producing more and more smoke as the music got faster,

until suddenly she
clapped her hands
and vanished
completely
– only to
reappear on
the other side
of the stage
without any
smoke around
her at all. Everyone
clapped and cheered.

Gina turned a cartwheel and then bowed
deeply.

Ellie, Summer and Jasmine cheered.

Gina held out her hands to them.
"Please, come and join me."

Jasmine and Ellie leapt on to the stage.
Summer hesitated. She was shyer than

the others and didn't really like lots of people watching her.

"Come on, Summer!" said Ellie, holding out her hand.

"You'll be brilliant!" Trixi whispered, flying by Summer's ear.

Summer took a deep breath and jumped on to the stage. Holding tightly to Ellie's hand, she ran to stand nervously behind Gina.

The genie clicked her fingers, and a long ribbon of bright pink smoke appeared. She handed it to Jasmine, who held it like a gymnast about to do a ribbon dance. Gina conjured two more smoke-streamers – yellow for Summer and purple for Ellie. "Dance with me, girls!" she cried.

The music started again. It seemed to

take hold of their feet, and even Summer
didn't have to worry about what she was
doing. The three of them twirled around
the stage with their smoke ribbons while
the audience clapped and cheered, and
King Merry even beat time on
a tambourine that Trixi had conjured
for him.

The girls danced until they were completely out of breath and then collapsed on a pile of silken cushions beside King Merry while Gina went to grant little wishes to people in the crowd.

Trixi conjured up glasses of the sweetest fruit punch imaginable. It tasted like mangoes and raspberries, and the glasses were magic – so no matter how much the girls drank they kept refilling!

"This is wonderful!" said Ellie. "Thanks, Trixi!"

Trixi kissed each of their noses. "I'm afraid it's time for you three to go home now," she said. "King Merry and I will take the Glitter Lamp back to the palace and keep it safe."

"We've just got one more Enchanted Object to find, and then we'll be able to stop Queen Malice's spell once and for all!" said Jasmine.

"I'll set to work finding out what the

last object is as soon as I get back to the palace," King Merry promised.

"And then we'll come back and help you find it," said Summer, giving him a big hug.

"Thank you, my dears, for everything you have done today," said the king. "I am sure I shall see you very soon."

The girls joined hands. "Bye, King Merry!" they called. "Bye Gina! Bye, everyone!"

Gina waved goodbye and the crowd cheered, then Trixi tapped her ring and the girls were whisked away.

They landed safely back in Ellie's bedroom, standing on the rug with the Magic Box between them. After being surrounded by music and cheering it felt very quiet and strange.

"It's nice to be home, but it seems so much less shiny here, doesn't it?" said Jasmine, looking round with a smile.

"The light was so bright in the Silver Desert," Summer agreed. "Everything seemed to glitter and sparkle."

"I hope we go somewhere just as exciting next time we visit the Secret Kingdom," said Ellie.

"Well, wherever we go, we'll find the last Enchanted Object and help King Merry stop Queen Malice!" declared Jasmine.

They all nodded. They were definitely going to do that. Very soon, they would be whisked to the Secret Kingdom again, off on another amazing adventure!

In the next Secret Kingdom
adventure, Ellie, Summer and
Jasmine search for the

Pixie Spell

Read on for a sneak peek...

A Garden
Riddle

"My project's going to be about deep-
sea creatures," said Ellie MacDonald
excitedly. She and her friends Summer
Hammond and Jasmine Smith were
doing their homework in Summer's living
room. They were working on projects
about animal habitats.

Ellie flipped through the book she'd been reading until she came to a picture showing whales, sharks and fish. "I'll be able to write about all of these." She glanced at Summer's two little brothers, Finn and Connor, who were playing at the other end of the room, then lowered her voice. "Too bad I can't write about mermaids, but Mrs Benson will think I'm making them up."

Jasmine looked up from the computer screen and grinned. "I'm doing my project on desert animals, like camels." She added in a whisper, "But not the pink ones we rode in the Secret Kingdom."

The girls smiled excitedly at each other, thinking about the amazing secret they all shared. They often visited a magical land called the Secret Kingdom. It was

ruled by kind King Merry and it was
full of fairies, pixies, dragons and other
wonderful creatures. During their last two
adventures there they'd made friends with
mermaids and ridden on pink camels!

"What habitat are you doing for your
project, Summer?" asked Jasmine.

Summer sighed. "I just can't decide."
She loved all animals and was finding it
impossible to choose.

Finn and Connor started arguing over
a train, shouting and snatching it from
each other. "Anyway," Summer said with
a giggle, "it's hard to think with those
two squabbling."

"I wish we could move to the garden,"
said Ellie. "It's more peaceful out there." It
was a beautiful summer's day and the girls
were all dressed in shorts and T-shirts.

Summer's mum came in. "Whatever's going on in here?" she asked.

"Connor snatched the train off me," moaned Finn.

"I had it first," Connor wailed.

"Take it in turns," said Mum. "Ten minutes each. When the timer pings, you swap." She set the timer on her phone. "You can have it first, Finn, and your time starts...now!"

The girls exchanged anxious looks.

"Are you thinking about Queen Malice's hourglass?" Jasmine whispered.

Summer and Ellie nodded. Queen Malice, King Merry's mean sister, had put a curse on the Secret Kingdom. As black sand ran through her hourglass, all the good magic was slowly being drained out of the kingdom. When all the sand was gone, the good magic would be lost forever – and Queen Malice would take over as ruler. The only way to lift the curse was by bringing four Enchanted Objects together again. The girls had already found three of them, but it hadn't been easy. King Merry's ancestors had hidden the Enchanted Objects well, to protect them.

"I wonder if King Merry's figured out where the last Enchanted Object is hidden," said Jasmine. It was still missing and time was running out!

"I wish Trixi would send us a message," said Summer. Their pixie friend, Trixi, sent them messages through their Magic Box when they were needed in the Secret Kingdom.

"Me, too," Ellie agreed. "Let's check the

Magic Box now."

"We're just having a quick break from our homework," Summer called to her mum.

The girls ran upstairs to Summer's bedroom.

Summer opened her wardrobe and a bright light shone out. "The Magic Box is glowing!" she cried excitedly. She lifted it out quickly and placed it on her desk. It was a wooden box, beautifully carved with mermaids, unicorns and other magical creatures. A mirror was set into the box's lid, surrounded by six green gems.

The girls crowded round the box eagerly and Ellie read out the words that had appeared on the glowing mirror:

"This magical place is very high.
It's full of ice and snow.
Pixies build cute snowmen there,
And that's where you must go."

The box flew open and a magical map of the Secret Kingdom floated out. Jasmine caught it and spread it out on the bed. Looking at the map was usually like peering through a window into the Secret Kingdom because the figures on it moved.

Read

Pixie Spell

to find out what
happens next!

Secret Kingdom

Have you read all the books in Series Seven?

Fairy Charm

ROSIE BANKS

Mermaid Magic

ROSIE BANKS

Genie Wish

ROSIE BANKS

Pixie Spell

ROSIE BANKS

When the last grain of sand falls in Queen
Malice's cursed hourglass, magic will be lost
from the Secret Kingdom forever!
Can Ellie, Summer and Jasmine find all the
Enchanted Objects and break the spell?

Secret Kingdom

Look out for the latest special!

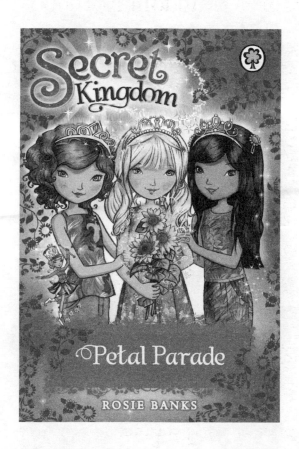

Out now!

Secret Kingdom

Queen Malice's spell on the Magic Hourglass is making everything in the Secret Kingdom go wonky!

Can you help the girls put things right by matching the picture with the right shadow?

Competition!

Those naughty Storm Sprites are up to no good again. They have trampled through this book and left muddy footprints on one of the pages!

Did you spot them while you were reading this book?

Can you find the pages where the cheeky sprites have left their footprints in each of the four books in series 7?
When you have found all four sets of footprints, go online and tell us which pages they are on to enter the competition at

www.secretkingdombooks.com

We will put all of the correct entries into a draw and select a winner to receive a special Secret Kingdom goody bag!

Alternatively send entries to:
Secret Kingdom, Series 7 Competition
Orchard Books, Carmelite House, 50 Victoria Embankment,
London, EC4Y 0DZ

Don't forget to add your name and address.

Good luck!

Closing date: 29th February 2016

Secret Kingdom

A magical world of
friendship and fun!

Join the Secret Kingdom Club at

www.secretkingdombooks.com

and enjoy games, sneak peeks and lots more!

You'll find great activities, competitions, stories
and games, plus a special newsletter for
Secret Kingdom friends!